# HE'S GOT the WHOLE WORLD in HIS HANDS

### KADIR NELSON

SCHOLASTIC INC.

# He's got the whole world in His hands,

He's got the whole world

in His hands,

He's got my **brothers** and
my **sisters** in His hands,

He's got the whole world

in His hands.

He's got the **sun** and the **rain** in His **hands,**

He's got the
moon and the stars
in His hands,

He's got the
wind and the clouds
in His hands,

He's got the
whole world
in His hands.

He's got the **rivers**
and the **mountains**
in His hands,

He's got the **oceans** and the **seas**
in His hands,

He's got **you**
and he's got **me**
in His hands,
He's got the
**whole**
**world**
in His hands.

He's got
**everybody**
**here**
in His
hands,

He's got everybody
there
in His hands,

He's got everybody
**everywhere**
in His hands,

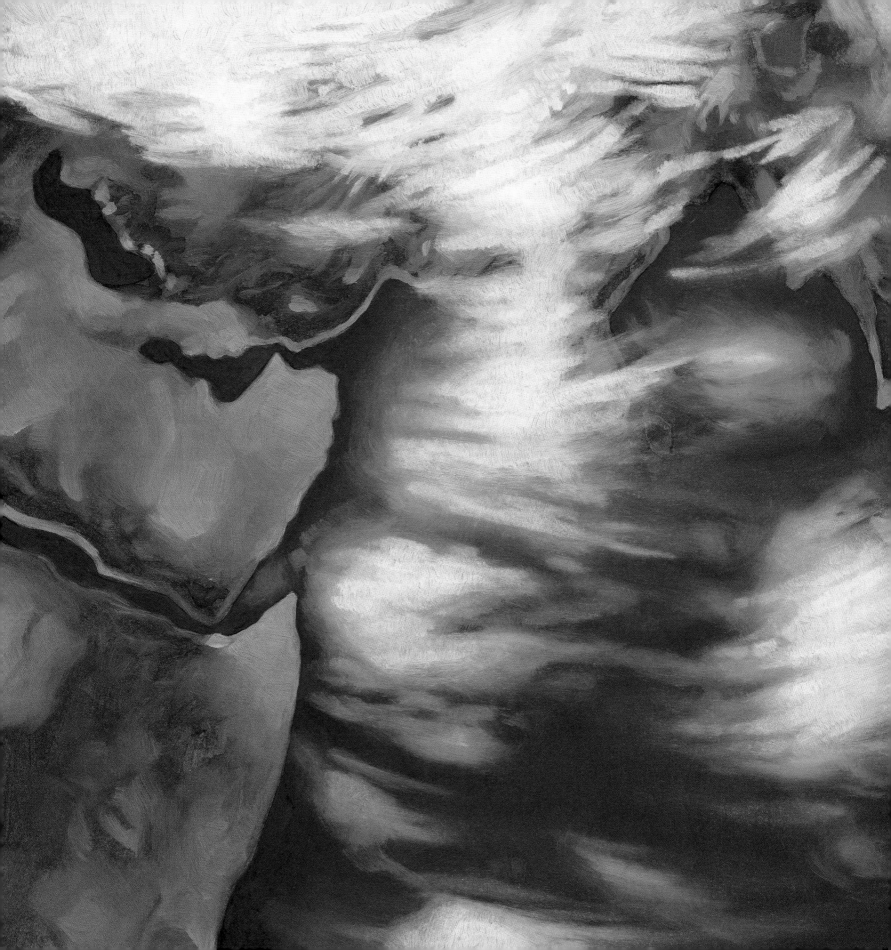

He's got the whole world in His hands.

2. He's got the sun and the rain in His hands,
   He's got the moon and the stars in His hands,
   He's got the wind and the clouds in His hands,
   He's got the whole world in His hands.

3. He's got the rivers and the mountains in His hands,
   He's got the oceans and the seas in His hands,
   He's got you and he's got me in His hands,
   He's got the whole world in His hands.

4. He's got everybody here in His hands,
   He's got everybody there in His hands,
   He's got everybody everywhere in His hands,
   He's got the whole world in His hands.

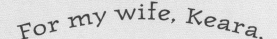

For my wife, Keara.

You mean the world to me. I love you dearly.

## A NOTE ABOUT THE SONG

The spiritual "He's Got the Whole World in His Hands" is one of the best-known songs of all time, sung at churches, schools, and camps throughout the country. Who created the first version of the folk song is unknown; often it is attributed simply to "various," as spirituals are songs that have been passed orally from person to person or group to group and improvised along the way. Now there are many versions of the lyrics; the ones chosen for this book may not exactly match those that you yourself know. But the mood and message—that of faith and the importance of community—are the same. The inspirational content of spirituals was crucial to the slaves who created them, and from this musical tradition was born gospel, blues, and jazz.

Over the years, "He's Got the Whole World in His Hands" has been recorded by numerous artists, from opera singer to country star to children's performer, including Marian Anderson, Perry Como, Odetta, Nina Simone, Mahalia Jackson, Loretta Lynn, and Raffi. It even became a number one pop single for a thirteen-year-old boy named Laurie London in 1958. Now this timeless song, still evolving, has also become a picture book.

ISBN 978-0-545-55090-1

12 11 10 9 8 7 6 5 4 3 2 1          13 14 15 16 17 18/0

Printed in the U.S.A.          08

This edition first printing, January 2013

Designed by Teresa Kietlinski
Music set by Robert L. Sherwin
Text set in Journal

The artwork for this book was created with pencil, oil, and watercolor. The kid-drawings were created by the artist (using his left hand) with colored pencils.